Written by Christa Carpenter

JILLI, THAT'S SILLY!

Illustrated by Mark Wayne Adams

Copyright © 2013 by Mark Wayne Adams, Inc.

Published by:

mwa

markwayneadams • inc

Contact Information:
Mark Wayne Adams, Inc.
Attn.: Mark Wayne Adams
P.O. Box 916392
Longwood, FL 32791-6392

Author: Christa Carpenter
Illustrator/Designer: Mark Wayne Adams
Editor: Jennifer Thomas

Christa Carpenter
First Edition

Library of Congress Control Number: 2012911511
ISBN-13: 978-1-59616-015-6
ISBN-10: 1-59616-015-02

First Printing 2013
Published in the United States of America
Printed in United States of America
Printer: Sprint Print, Inc.

Jillian Wallaby was always doing
silly things!
And her mom was always letting her know...

1

Jilli, that's silly!

2

You're just seven—not twenty-two.
Those clothes are way too BIG for you!

3

Jilli, that's silly!

4

You're perfect as you are.
Slow down, my sweet girl.
In time, you'll be a star.

5

Jilli, that's silly!

6

We have lots of places to go.
We don't need another baby in tow.

A book, *MY* lipstick, a scarf and comb—
can't you leave some of this at home?

9

These things are used inside.

"But I NEED them for my kitchen, Mom!" is all Jilli replied.

Jilli, that's silly!

You've been on that phone all day.
There is no one on the other end.
What COULD you have to say?

You're not a mom just yet.
You're still my little girl
—don't you forget!

15

16

Why, they are just a dog and cat.
Do you think they prefer
to dress like that?

17

That night, when Jilli's mom brushed her hair before bed, this is what she said:

Today, Jilli...

19

You've worn my clothes
half falling down,

20

and sang like a rock star touring the town.

21

Your baby came along
with all her **stuff**,

22

and that little Purse of yours
held quite enough.

You set up house outside,
kitchen and all,

24

and then spent the day on one **long** phone call.

You bossed your brother just like a mom would,

26

and dressed doggy and kitty in a coat and hood.

But, my oh my, has this day been a WHIRL! So...

Jilli, that's NOT silly!

That's just being a GIRL!

30

Book Talk

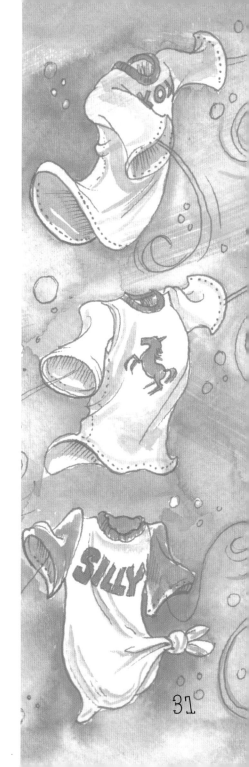

1. How would you define the word "silly"?

2. Describe a time when you acted silly. Did you get in trouble for acting silly?

3. Whom do you know that reminds you of Jilli?

4. Sometimes adults forget how to act "silly." Why do you think this happens?

5. Do you think you could teach an adult how to act silly? How would you do it?

6. If you could get away with doing one really silly thing, what would it be?

7. What was your favorite "silly" thing that Jilli did? Why?

8. What other "silly" things can you find happening in the book?

9. Why do you think Jilli's mom realized in the end that it was okay to be silly?

10. Would you like to be friends with Jilli? Why or why not?

Continue your collection with Christa's other books!

Nicholas, That's Ridiculous!

Nicholas Wallaby was always doing ridiculous things! And his mom was always letting him know. "Nicholas, That's Ridiculous!" she'd say—at least thirty times a day. Finally, Nicholas's mom realizes that Nicholas *isn't* being ridiculous—he's just being a boy!

Jilli, That's Silly!

Jillian Wallaby was always doing silly things! And her mom was always letting her know. "Jilli That's Silly!" she'd repeat, over and over without skipping a beat. Finally, Jilli's mom realizes that Jilli *isn't* being silly—she's just being a girl!

Eddie, That's Spaghetti!

Eddie Wallaby was always trying to sneak the Sunday dinner. And his family was always telling him no. "Eddie, That's Spaghetti!" they'd say, and then try to distract him in another way. Finally, Eddie's family agrees that Eddie isn't being a hog—he's just being a dog!

Each book includes a BOOK TALK
to engage children in discussion,
imagination, and perception.

Produced by award-winning publisher
Mark Wayne Adams, Inc.

ORDER at WWW.markwayneadams.com OR anywhere fine books are SOLD!

Award-winning Author · Illustrator · Publisher
Mark Wayne Adams

Mark Wayne Adams is an award-winning illustrator, author, and publisher who has illustrated over thirty-two children's books in the past six years. As a public speaker, he uses his talents to inspire others through reading, writing, and art. He received the annual Marlene M. Helm Alumni Achievement Award for his contribution to the arts and his dedication to enriching Kentucky's artistic future.

Mark resides in Longwood, Florida, with his wife, Angela, his two children, Isabella and Carter, and their dogs, Russell and Libbi.

Moonbeam Children's Book Award · Independent Publisher Book Award · Florida Publishers Association Award · Eric Hoffer Award

Award-winning Author
Christa Carpenter

Christa Carpenter is a mother of two wonderful children who inspire her to write. She enjoys teaching first-graders to be leaders using Dr. Stephen Covey's 7 Habits of Happy Kids. *Jilli, That's Silly* is her second published picture book. Her first in the series, *Nicholas, That's Ridiculous!*, has won four awards: the Florida Publishers Association President's Award, the Moonbeam Children's Book Award, the IPPY Award, and the Eric Hoffer Award.

Christa lives in Florida with her son and daughter, Nicholas and Jillian, their funny dog, Eddie, and their clever cat, Rex.

33

To all the "silly" girls in my life. Especially...

Jillian—you have taught me to not take myself so seriously.

You are the light of my life!